ANOTHER PERFECT DAY

ROSS MACDONALD

ROARING BROOK PRESS
Brookfield, Connecticut

For Jamie, Daisy, and Lucy

A NEAL PORTER BOOK

Copyright©2002 by Ross MacDonald

Published by Roaring Brook Press
A division of The Millbrook Press, 2 Old New Milford Road, Brookfield, Connecticut 06804

Library of Congress Cataloging-in-Publication Data
MacDonald, Ross.
Another perfect day / by Ross MacDonald. 1st ed.
p.   cm.
Summary: What started out as another perfect day for a superhero performing heroic feats suddenly goes awry.
[1. Heroes Fiction.] I. Title.
PZ7.M1513 An 2002
[E] dc21   2002018798

0-7613-1595-0 (trade)
2 4 6 8 10 9 7 5 3 1

0-7613-2659-6 (library binding)
2 4 6 8 10 9 7 5 3 1

Printed in the United States of America
First edition

The morning sun came streaming through Jack's bedroom window.

He got
up and
looked
out . . .

got dressed . . .

ate breakfast . . .

brushed his teeth . . .

exercised . . .

and went out.

He stopped
to help out
here . . .

and there . . .

but by now
he was
running
late . . .

so he
caught
the train . . .

to work.

After work
he decided
to walk home.

they didn't.

In fact, things started to go a little funny.

He went to get his plane . . .
but it looked a little
funny, too!

So, Jack tried
everything . . .

splashing water on his face . . .

an alarm clock. . . .

EVERYTHING!

And sure enough . . .

when Jack tried it . . .

he woke up!